THIS IS A HOUSE

THIS IS A HOUSE

Colleen Stanley Bare
Photographs by the author

COBBLEHILL BOOKS
Dutton · New York

To Mike

Library of Congress Cataloging-in-Publication Data

Bare, Colleen Stanley.
This is a house / Colleen Stanley Bare ; photographs by the author.
p. cm.
Includes index.
Summary: Follows, in text and photographs, the building of a house from the architectural plans to moving-in day.
ISBN 0-525-65090-3
1. House construction—Juvenile literature. [1. House construction.] I. Title.
TH4811.5.B36 1992
690'.89—dc20 91-28192 CIP AC

Published in the United States by Cobblehill Books,
an affiliate of Dutton Children's Books,
a division of Penguin Books USA Inc.
375 Hudson Street, New York, New York 10014

Designed by Charlotte Staub
Printed in Hong Kong First Edition
10 9 8 7 6 5 4 3 2 1

This is the plan that an architect made for a house being built on a hilltop lot.

Here is a machine,
a bulldozer that clears the land.

It scoops out dirt and rocks and sand, so
the boundaries of the plan can be outlined
in smooth soil of the hilltop plot.

The carpenters dig trenches in the shape of the house and line the sides of the trenches with wooden boards, called *forms.*

Steel rods are placed inside the forms, and concrete is poured over the steel rods.

The concrete poured into the wooden forms works like gelatin in a mold. When the concrete hardens and the forms are removed, what is left is the *foundation* that will hold up the house.

Also part of the foundation are thirty *footings* that help to support the house and act like feet. Placed in the ground, they are made of concrete.

Now on top of the foundation
are bolted some boards,

and on top of the footings are nailed some posts,

and on top of the bolted boards and the posts are nailed rows of thick big beams called *floor joists.*

The carpenters are a busy bunch, all day lifting, measuring, pounding, sawing, nailing, with a short break for lunch.
They will use 400 pounds of nails to build this house.

This is the *subfloor* the carpenters build, which they glue and nail to the floor joists.

The subfloor is 56 sheets of plywood, 3/4 inch thick, each sheet four feet by eight feet.

When finished the subfloor is flat, smooth, and neat, and the underneath part of the house is complete.

Next come the walls of the house which are like a skeleton. The vertical (up and down) bones are pieces of lumber called *studs.* They are laid out on the subfloor and nailed together.

Now the studs are lifted into place and nailed to the subfloor, to form the walls of the house.

Other bones in the skeleton are *ceiling joists.* These are horizontal (sideways) boards that hold up the ceiling.

The process of building the skeleton has a name: *framing,* or *to frame.*

High windows are framed by surefooted carpenters.

The studs around the house on the outside are covered with heavy moistureproof paper called *sheathing.* Spaces are cut out for the windows and doors.

One hundred panels of wood *siding* are nailed on the outside of the house, over the studs and paper sheathing. This becomes the outer skin of the house. Some houses have outer skins of brick, stone, or stucco, instead of the wood.

Now that the bottom and sides of the house are finished (foundation, subfloor, skeleton walls, and siding), it is time to build the top of the house. The top of the house is the roof and its supports. The supports come first, called *rafters* or *trusses.*

These are the trusses, being moved V-E-R-Y carefully, and nailed onto the tops of the walls.

One slip and, oops, big trouble!

Eighty-five plywood panels are nailed to the trusses, to form the *subroof.*

These are the roofers putting black felt roofing paper on top of the subroof—and fireproof fiberglass shingles on top of the roofing paper. Some houses have shingles of wood, metal, or tile, instead of the fiberglass.

Other kinds of workers are also busy. Electricians provide electric power for lights and plugs. Here is the metal service box they install, to carry electricity from the power company to the house.

Electric wires are run from the metal box into switch boxes placed between wall studs and in ceilings.

Plumbers and heating experts put water pipes, gas pipes, and sewer pipes in walls and under floors.

These inside pipes are attached to outside pipes, buried in trenches. The outside pipes are connected to the community's water, gas, and sewer systems.

Now, through the water pipes, the house will get fresh water for drinking, cooking, and bathing; through the gas pipes, the house will get gas to run the furnace; and through the sewer pipes, it will get rid of waste from toilets, tubs, showers, and sinks.

A bathtub and shower are put in place by the plumber.

Insulation installers put insulation between wall studs, between the joists under the floor, and in the attic above the ceiling—to keep out the cold and keep in the heat in winter, and to keep out the heat and keep in the cool in summer.

Next, *drywall* is nailed to the skeleton walls.

Drywall is panels of plaster covered with heavy paper. Holes are cut in the drywall for the plumbing, electric switch boxes, and lights.

No longer can you see the studs, wiring, or plumbing pipes.

The painter puts two coats of paint on the drywall.

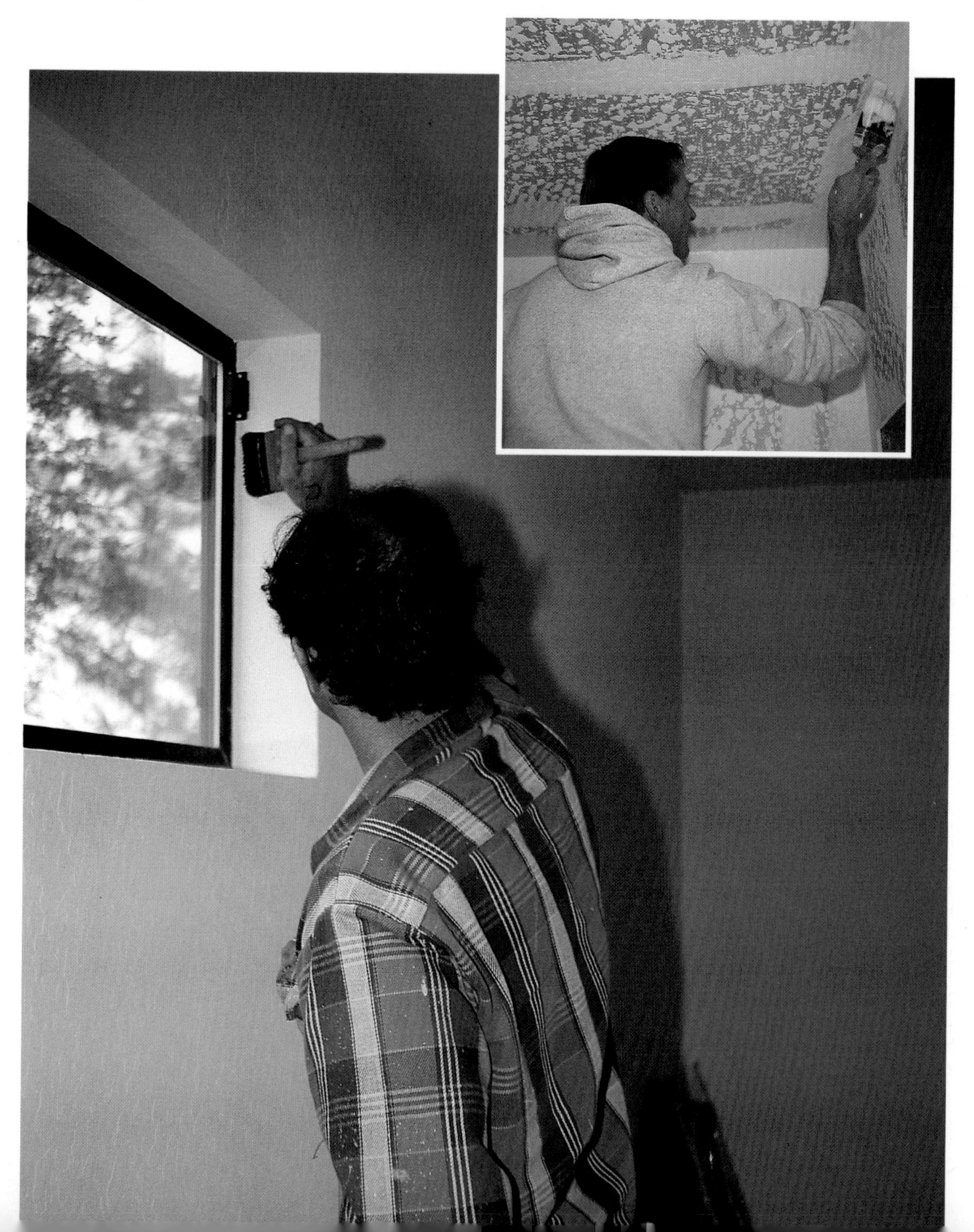

At last the house is almost finished.

The cabinetmaker delivers the cabinets, and flooring people install carpet and vinyl on the floors.

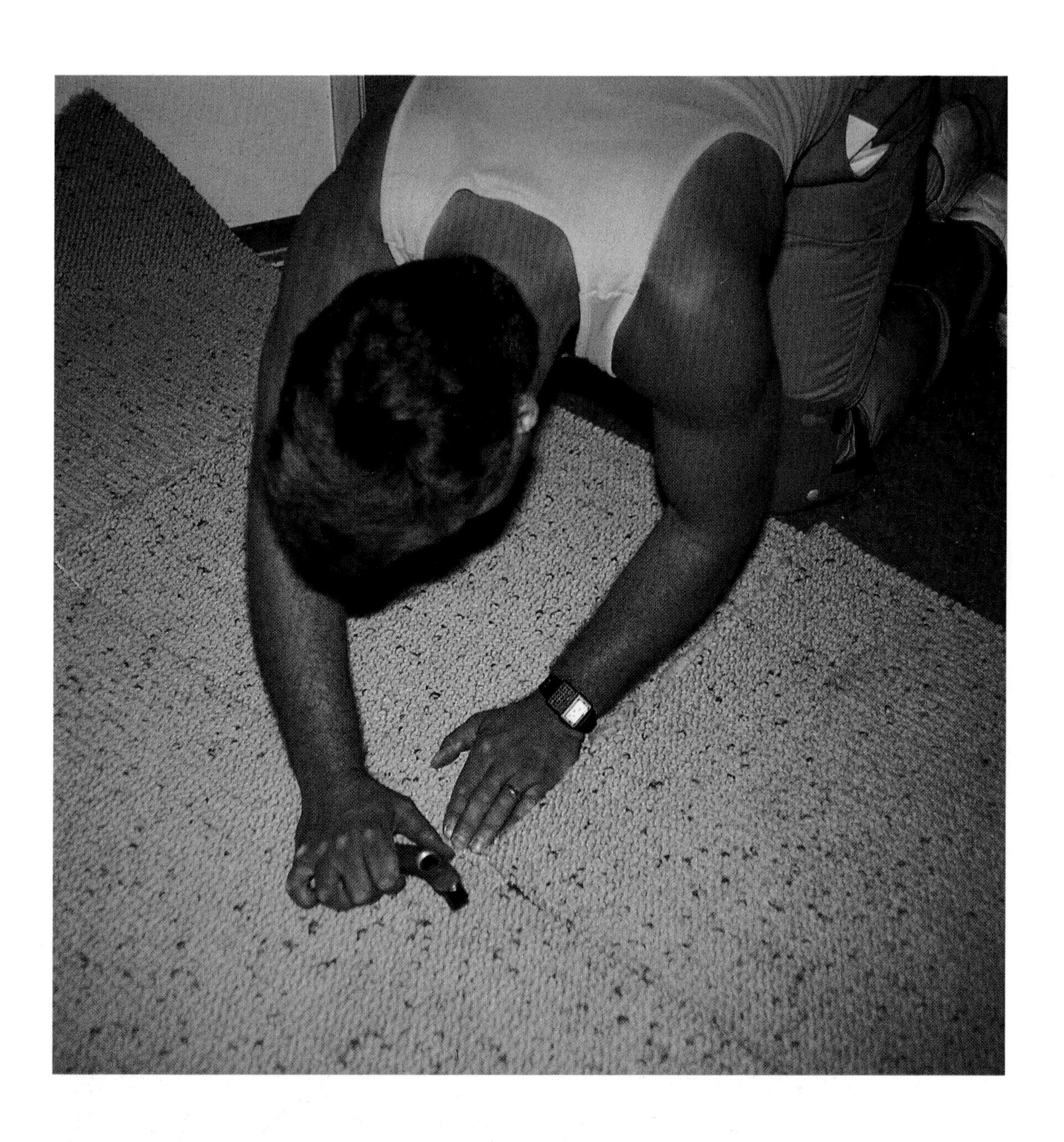

The carpenters hang 11 doors, with
11 doorknobs and 33 hinges; the
electrician installs 20 light fixtures,
35 plugs, and 26 switches; the
heating man connects the furnace,

and the plumber puts
in toilets, sinks,
and faucets.

One day a moving van arrives, bringing furniture into the sparkling new rooms.

This is the house that now is a home.

HOUSE WORDS

For Those Who Want to Know More

architect A person who designs houses and draws house plans.

attic Space above the ceiling and the underside of the roof.

beam A long piece of wood or metal that supports a heavy load and often covers a wide distance.

concrete A building material made up of fine and coarse rock, sand, and water bonded together by cement.

drywall An interior wall covering, also called wallboard or by the brand name Sheetrock. It usually comes in large sheets and is made of plaster covered with heavy paper. A special material called *spackle* is used to hide the seams.

electric service panel A metal box, usually mounted on an outer wall of the house, containing wires that bring the electricity into the house.

footings Supports in the ground, often concrete, that help carry the weight of the house.

foundation The framework and building materials below the ground floor, including the footings, that support the house.

framing The skeleton of the exterior and interior walls, including doors and windows.

insulation Material used to protect a house from heat and cooling loss. Examples are fiberglass batting for walls and floors, blown-in fiberglass or cellulose materials in attics, fiberglass insulation on roofs, and windows built with pockets of air between two layers of glass.

joists Horizontal (sideways) pieces of lumber used to support floors and ceilings.

lumber Wood milled into specific shapes, such as 1×4, 2×4, 3×4, etc.

nails Slender, rigid rods of metal, pointed at one end and flattened at the other. They come in many standard sizes and are used to join together pieces of lumber, usually with a hammer.

paper sheathing A layer of paper or film, applied to the studs, to keep out air, wind, and moisture.

plans Drawings that show where a house is to be placed on a lot and the interior layout of the rooms, walls, doors, utilities, etc.

plywood Wood made of three or more layers of wood joined together by glue, with the grain in different directions. Four-by-eight-foot sheets of plywood paneling are often used for subfloors, subroofs, and siding.

rafters The wood framework designed to support the weight of the roof. Trusses do the same thing.

roofing paper Heavy paper, also called **roof felting**, applied to the subroof before laying down the shingles.

shingles The covering for a roof made of wood, fiberglass, tile or metal.

siding The outside covering of the house. It may be plywood panels, boards, shingles, stucco, or metal.

steel rods Often called **reinforcing steel bars** or **rebars**, these are steel rods placed in concrete to make the concrete stronger—used especially for foundations, garages, walks, driveways, and porches.

stud Vertical (up and down) lumber that supports the walls, ceilings, and roof.

subfloor A layer of boards or plywood nailed and/or glued to the floor joists, later covered by the finished floor of carpet, vinyl, tile, hardwood, etc.

subroof Plywood panels, usually four feet by eight feet, nailed on top of the trusses. Felt and shingles are then applied to this subroof.

truss A rigid framework, often factory-built, designed to support a wide distance such as the weight of a roof. Rafters do the same.

INDEX